Thalia

and The Purity Virtue

By
Rozl Lee

LBP

www.thelionsbrood.com

First printing, first edition

ISBN: 978-1-7363861-2-5
PUBLISHED BY LION'S BROOD PUBLISHING, LLC
www.thelionsbrood.com

Printed in the United States of America

1.

Wake, Young One

You are the daughter to the Sun. You are daughter to the Earth. You are sibling to the Moon. Destiny awaits you. Find your strength within, young child. The world is yours to care for and protect. You are its protector from all that would do it harm. Your powers are omnipotent. Discover the purity from whence it thrives. Like a river that flows in all directions, go with the wind. Let it take you to untold wonders.

Let the sun warm your back, knowing he will always guide you home to where you belong. He is never out of reach. I'm here for you. The very ground trembles under your wake. Let it embrace you.

The *Spirit of Kalas* growls for the truth to be told. Care for those around you, even when they doubt your sincerity. The universe owes you everything. The world owes you nothing. Take heed, for fortunes are not guaranteed or welcomed in this careless life they call existence.

Follow what you know holds true in life and in futility. And never forget, you are immortal with the blood of yesterday flowing through your veins. Born with the gods at your side, always remember you bleed as though you are man. Your wisdom has carried for 8,000 years, and now your journey begins. Come home, young one. For you are Thalia, last of our kind.

The song is written, sing for everyone to hear. Let the melody capture and wrap those that listen. Never forget, you are not alone. Your father watches with a discerning gaze. This undeserving earth is unforgiving. Home is from where you came. Descendent of the heavens, carrier of the truth. Adventure awaits you. Are you afraid? Do not be. The blood of the spirits will guide you to your destination.

2.

Spirit of Kalas

Gaia and her elite guards braced themselves for another onslaught by Enlil and his Elements. Darkness filled the sky as storm clouds covered and loomed over the mountainous terrain. Heavy rain and lightening warned Mother Earth and the soldiers lined behind her of the enemy's attack.

Clenching her long spear, Gaia fastened her bronze helmet over her flowing reddish-brown hair. The six-foot-tall spear matched her height, and the spearhead glistened even without sunlight. Her calming gaze surveyed the moss-covered landscape; she was unfazed by the ominous thunder.

"Prepare yourselves, servants of Earth. The future is in your hands," Gaia screamed to her guards as she mounted her large bull with fierce horns.

The soldiers readied their swords and halberds after hearing her words of motivation. Bronze helmets and armor covered their stone frames. They were soldiers made of the very earth they protected. Only their glowing eyes under the shadow of their helmets showed they were living creatures.

A strong wind swept past Gaia as she lowered her spear and commanded her mount to a slow gallop. Her soldiers marched behind her. The heavy footsteps of an army numbering a thousand rattled the ground, causing small animals in the area to flee in a panic. Soon, thousands of ghostly humanoid forms appeared in the distance and let out a horrific shriek as they flew above the ground towards Gaia's army.

"Fight until none of these wretched creatures remain!" Gaia lifted her spear as her gigantic mount charged ahead to meet the faceless horde. Her soldiers followed suit with their shields and weapons extended. Lightening crackled above the battlefield.

The two armies clashed. The sound of blades slashing the air and gusts of damaging wind pummeled the rocky soldiers. With each swing of their fists, the Elements inflicted a concussive force on unprotected soldiers. The blow shattered the first line of soldiers; their earthly forms became dust and dissolved with the wind. As the soldiers retaliated with weapon strikes, several of the Elements changed from gas to liquid and were lost in the rain. Gaia enchanted the soldiers' blades before the battle, enabling the weapons to wound the otherwise indestructible Elements.

Enlil, standing on a dark cloud, swooped down from the sky. He was a giant of sorts, standing seven-foot tall. His eyes glowed brighter in anticipation of battle. As he lowered himself to the ground before Gaia, his azure cloak ruffled in the wind. Enlil extended his long staff and twirled it with great speed, shooting intense gusts at Gaia. The concussive wind knocked Gaia from her bull. She rolled on the grassy plain until coming to her feet with spear in hand.

"You grow weaker with each battle, sister," Enlil shouted as he moved to within ten feet of Gaia. Raindrops trickled down his short, reddish-brown hair and his colorless face.

"And you grow more foolish each time I face you, younger brother!" Gaia launched her spear at Enlil with the force of a thousand eagles in flight.

"Hardly." Enlil dodged the missile with ease by hovering above its path. "It is you who is the fool, my sister." He darted towards Gaia; the air beneath him parted with intensity.

Just before Enlil swung his staff at Gaia's head, Gaia's spear flew back to her hand. Their poles clashed, emitting a brilliant flash of energy. Gaia repelled his downward strike and kicked Enlil in his stomach, causing him to tumble several feet backwards. As he regained his footing, Gaia knelt and clenched the ground, inserting her fingers into the moist earth. The ground rumbled, and in an instant, the earth rose, sending a wave of soil and boulders towards Enlil. Before the rocks could crush her rival, Enlil leaped into the sky and retaliated with a lightening bolt from his hand.

White flames struck Gaia's armor and knocked her off her feet. Enlil sent another bolt her direction, but Gaia commanded the earth before her to lift, which shielded her from the strike. The wall of dirt and boulders shattered but protected Gaia nonetheless.

As Gaia raised her arms into the air, the surrounding mountains rose in height. The sky became covered in darkness.

"I will destroy you if it's my last breath," Gaia announced.

"It is you I do not want. Be kind and hand over Thalia," Enlil screamed. "I know your plan. Don't you understand? She cannot succeed. She will erase us all."

"She is our last hope of existence, yet you would see her downfall. She is of your spirit!"

Enlil lowered himself to the ground and

unsheathed his blade. "It means nothing if I must rid ourselves of the self-destructive humans." He launched himself at Gaia with the cry of a heavy gust of wind.

Two of Gaia's stone soldiers shielded Gaia from Enlil's sword thrust. They quickly became a mist of dust and gas.

Thalia gazed at her reflection in the Pond of Sincerity. Her almond-shaped eyes sparkled in the bright blue waters. She stood around five feet and four inches, which is not obvious since she was kneeling. Her decorative tunic remained unsoiled and pristine.

"What are you looking for?"

The voice came from over her shoulder.

Thalia's stare remained on the pond. "How often does one get to see themselves for what they are inside?" Thalia let her fingers stroke the water. Gently, she let her fingers become wet with curiosity.

"You make me laugh, Little One," Twilight the cat echoed without moving her furry lips. "You look for what you know is true, but you expect to see the unexpected. Why do you look for more than what is before you?" Twilight was Abyssinian in breed. Her short hair glistened under the sunlight. Her light and dark, fawn hue and pointed ears presented a regal appearance.

"Maybe I want to see what lies underneath it all," Thalia muttered under her voice. To look upon Thalia, one would assume she was a normal child of 14 years of age. They would be mistaken. It would be more accurate to know she was about 5,000 years old. Just a youth in her species.

Thalia rose to her feet. "You are so

skeptical. I suppose it's because you're a cat." She smiled at her feline companion. "You are too untrusting of the soul for your own good," Thalia laughed while brushing aside her long, dark hair.

"I live in a world of reality," Twilight responded while licking her paws.

The small projectile ricochetted off Thalia's forehead.

"*Kalas' Spirit*!" screamed Thalia. She rubbed the struck area. "What was that?"

Twilight approached the white projectile on the ground and started sniffing it. "It looks like a combination of balled paper with the saliva of a person. It seems that Celio has awakened from his slumber," Twilight estimated. "It came from the forest beyond."

"That little *blolock*," Thalia said.

"It is what the dwellers of this world refers

to as a spit-ball," Twilight added.

Thalia immediately dashed into the thick forest. Her eyesight pierced her surroundings. There was an eerie silence, except the chirping of an occasional songbird bringing in the early morning. Thalia was very familiar with the flora since she and Celio played among these trees in the past. He was still just as annoying as ever before.

"Where are you, Celio? You can't hide for long." Thalia scanned the forest as she walked deeper into its shade. "You've never been cunning in a game of hide and find."

Thalia could see Celio hunched down inside a blackberry bush, but she pretended not to see him. Thalia stopped and decided to have a little fun with her little brother.
"Oh well, I guess he disappeared," Thalia sighed

as she slowly walked the other direction. Out of her side-vision she could see a petite figure sprint from one bush to another. Thalia stared at the ground. Several lizards were scurrying across the dirt floor, looking for sunlight to warm themselves from the frigid shaded forest. "What are these? I've never seen these kinds of lizards in this world."

Suddenly, Celio ran up to his big sister. He stood slightly shorter than Thalia, about five feet tall and thin. His prickly, low haircut blended well with his beige complexion. To look upon him, you would think he was nine years old. Of course, like Thalia, age appearances were deceiving for his people. He knelt in front of her with his permanent smirk and grabbed one of the lizards.

"This is a Gecko lizard. Don't you know anything, Thalia?"

"I know you're the most gullible brother in the family," Thalia chuckled as she gently tapped Celio on the pate of his head.

"Ouch, that hurt!" Celio said.

"No. it didn't, you little bug."

Celio was quite the mischievous one. He wasn't a bad prince necessarily, but his curiosity often landed him in trouble with Gaia, his mother. What Thalia finds humorsome and frustrating about Celio is that he has a keen memory, yet he makes the same mistakes twice.

Celio stands. "I just wrote another story for Father."

"Is that so?" Thalia replied.

Celio lowered his head. "I think he will like it." Celio wiped his eyes. "I miss him."

"So do I." Thalia said. She stares into the sunlight. "He would want us to carry on. Protect

Mother."

Thalia extends her index finger and a monarch butterfly lands on it. "To think, this will all be mine someday. I will rule as Father did, with kindness."

It was as though Thalia was one with nature and all living creatures...except humans. She was never permitted to interact with their species. Although they shared the same world, Gaia and Nuru would never allow their children to interfere with the strifes of humanity.

The butterfly flew away. "We must ask Lady Maiden to tell us human stories after lessons. What book are you reading today?" Thalia said.

"It is very interesting. The story of a great human king, Celio said. "His name is Gilgamesh. He wanted to become like us but never achieved it. He ruled the Kingdom of Uruk."

"Why would he want to be something that he is not? What a burden," Thalia interjected.

"I don't know. Sad he finished his days wandering some forest. He just could not stay awake," Celio said.

Twilight ran up and perched herself on the tallest nearby stone. Her tail dangled from left to right. Suddenly, the skies became cloudy and grey. Thunder echoed in the distance.

"A battle has ensued," Twilight said. " Your uncle is still up to his treachery."

Out of the earth, Gaia rose with her arms folded. She wore an azure cloak, which complemented her long, reddish-brown hair. Her eyes maintained a certain calmness.

"Mother!" Celio said as he ran and hugged his mother by the waistline.

Gaia smiled as she gazed upon her son.

"Celio. How is my playful prince?" She returned the embrace.

"Read a new story," Celio proclaimed.

"Is that so?" Gaia then stared at Thalia.

"Mother, is everything okay?" Thalia said.

"Thalia, come with me," Gaia said in a monotone voice. "The time has come."

3.

The Unravelling

Enlil's dwelling existed in the clouds--one particular dark cloud that blocked the very sun. Surrounded by darkness with the occasional torchlight, he sat upon his crystal throne. Stroking his goatee, he espied his surroundings. Before him knelt three *wisps*. They were translucent in appearance and were humanoid form but had no facial features. To the unsuspecting, they were identical.

"Have you not destroyed Gaia?" The three wisps said simultaneously.

"You would have me destroy my only sibling?" Enlil whispered as he ceased caressing his beard.

"No, my lord," The wisps spoke in unison. "However, time is of the essence."

"The humans seek to destroy this world for which we share," Enlil continued. "They should be washed away from this world. Prophecy commands that they be no more."

"It is very possible, my lord," said in unison. "However, if they should uncover the scrolls-"

"An impossibility of reason. As long as I continue the destruction of the humans, Gaia must remain in their defense, and the scrolls exist in the past. She grows weaker with each encounter."

"The wisps stare at each other for a moment then return their attention to their master. "A very wise decision, my lord," the wisps responded. "However, another can recover the *Scrolls of Virtue*. Perhaps she will recruit someone close to her to recover them in her stead."

Enlil's eyes glowed bright as frustration set in. He stood and loomed over the wisps. His lips curled with great disdain. Slowly, he approached the wisps, his long, azure cape flapped behind him. A strong wind swept through the chamber and silence grew heavy.

"Since Nuru's demise, there is none capable of retrieving the scrolls without Gaia's help," Enlil said as he stared downward at his benevolent retainers.

"There is one, my lord," the wisps said in unison and hesitantly. "Your niece. She carries the Spirit of Kalas in her."

"Thalia? Is that so? It seems my niece is more than a pretty face," Enlil said.

"It would appear so."

"Shame I must rip her apart," Enlil added.

"You must do what destiny demands, my lord," the wisps prostrated before Enlil.

"Bring her to me. Soul intact or not."

Gaia and Thalia walked along their plane of existence. It was a world covered with flora and fauna. Streams cut through the sea of green, giving way to the sunbeams that streamed from above the horizon. As Gaia gazed upon her daughter, she remembered when she met Nuru in a meadow just like this. "This was once a peaceful kingdom...until Enlil's betrayal."

"Always remember that your father shines upon you, always," Gaia said.

Thalia looked up. "What happened to Father?"

"He dwells in the universe and is captured within the sun. In a moment of jealousy, he was casted away. One day, he will return to us. I will tell you more when you return. I promise," Gaia said with a smile.

Thalia restrained herself from asking more from her mother. She knew time had a place at this moment. Until then, she must wait for her father's return.

Gaia continued, "In many ways, we are not so different from the humans. When Kalas settled our people on this world, we agreed to share all it had to offer. Thousands of years has passed, and we remain separate from the strifes of humanity. They cannot see us. They cannot hear us."

"Is that so?" Gaia contemplated.

"We are superior to humankind. Our ability to become one with our spirituality poses a great danger to them," Gaia added. "Kalas understood this. For thousands of years, we have lived side-by-side."

"Why can't we live together as one? Maybe we can teach them a better way?" Thalia pondered.

"I will show you why, my love."

Gaia raised her right palm, and their surroundings transformed into a world Thalia had never seen. It became a background of automobiles, crowds of people walking to their destination, and factories spewing gaseous clouds into the Earth's sky. The pollution surprised Thalia immediately.

"I have hidden their true world from you for thousands of years," Gaia said. "For millions of their years, the humans once lived as we do today until machines and vices took over their very existence. This is their world."

Thalia stepped away and stared at her surroundings. "They choose to live in this kind of world?"

"They are aware of its dangers and choose to do nothing about it. They are destroying their world--our world. Somewhere, they lost their way," Thalia surmised. "You must save the world before it is no more."

"What can I do?" Thalia said as she became nervous without understanding the reason for this inner-feeling.

Gaia stopped walking and gazed at her daughter. Her face became stern, announcing the seriousness of the situation. "We must uncover the eight Scrolls of Virtue to set the world back to its proper place. We must bring the scrolls from the past to the present."

"I can travel to the past?" Thalia scanned her frail figure.

"You can," Gaia said, "with the *Necklace of*

Daichi, sent to us from the essence of Kalas. It was a gift to me from Nuru upon our joining."

Gaia took the necklace off her neck and put it around Thalia's neck. Thalia admired the relic as one would admire a star in the night sky. Its majestic beauty was a hue Thalia had never witnessed. Embedded within its center were four stones.

Gaia caressed the gems. "Each stone represents a part of our original home. This is the *Vulcan Stone*. It provides a beam of protection. This is the *Kai Stone*. With this stone, you will be able to communicate with anyone, regardless of their native tongue. This is the *Chi Stone*. It will give you nourishment. And this is the *Dalibor Stone*. The most precious of them all. It will allow you to travel to any point in time."

"How do I know which time to travel? The

scrolls could be anywhere...anytime."

"The stone will guide you. Follow it. It is in tune with the scrolls." Gaia held Thalia by the shoulders. "I know you are afraid. Do not be. Destiny has spoken and you will fulfill yours."

"I will have to leave you. What of Celio and Twilight? What is to become of them?" Thalia cried out.

"They will remain to help me protect our realm. They will be waiting when you return." Gaia spoke with an uneasy confidence. "Just remember...your father will always guide you."

"Will the others know what I do for our people?" Thalia began to cry.

A tear ran down Gaia's cheek. "They will know that you are our savior. So young, yet so brave. They will be proud to call you princess."

Thunder began to angrily disperse above

them. Gaia rose from kneeling and look to the sky. Suddenly, her robe changed to golden armor covered by an azure cloak. She unsheathed a broadsword.

"Enlil is here. You must go!"

"Go where?" Thalia said. "The stone said nothing."

"Go to the Pond of Sincerity. There you will find the gateway to the past," Gaia shouted.

Thalia ran six feet away, only to return to embrace her mother. "I will not fail you, Mother." Thalia stated with absolution. Thalia then dashed to the forest, her hair long, flowing hair fluttered in the storm breeze.

Enlil and his Elementals flew above the small kingdom. Tornado winds swirled in the sky. Trees cracked under the enormous pressure and flocks of songbirds fled in fear. Drenching rain fell upon *Marlet Kingdom.* Deer trampled the grassy floor beneath them.

Gaia hovered above the clearing and raised both arms. Her army of stone warriors fired arrows into the sky as the wind transformed into a giant sandstorm.

"So you're sending the girl to steal what belongs to me!" Enlil yelled against the high winds. The sand blinded his vision. Several of the Elements slowly dissipated while being pummeled by sand.

"She is of your spirit yet you want her destroyed," Gaia screamed. "How can you be such a bitter soul?"

"I will find her! I will track her, find her, and destroy my niece! Do you hear me? For all that holds true, I swear by Kalas, she will fail," Enlil said with rage as his eyes glowed crimson. "Thalia will not rid me of my destiny!"

Gaia let out a slight smirk. "Enlil, you fool. Can't you see she has already succeeded?"

Enlil wore an inquisitive stare as his brow crinkled in disgust.

Through the swirling winds, Thalia dashed through the forest. She breathed heavily, wishing she had the speed of her brother. Vegetation gave way to the Pond of Sincerity. The waters had large waves created by Enlil's relentless zephyrs.

Thalia tripped and fell along the banks of the pond. Suddenly she heard a ghostly voice.

"You must go deep into the pond's depths."

The voice resonated within her mind, catching her off-guard.

"The Dalibor Stone," Thalia realized. "It's

talking to me."

That's when she noticed the stone sparkled with an illustrious glow. She held the necklace and regained her feet. Her tunic remained unsoiled. Thalia let go of the necklace and sprinted towards the pond. The air cut through her very being, and her eyes began to water.

"It will not be that simple, young one," came the voices.

Thalia stopped in her tracks. Nervously, she espied her surroundings when a translucent figure materialized in front of her. Immediately, two more of these figures appeared on both sides of the youth.

"Who are you?" Thalia screamed. Her heart pounded with fear.

"Matters not," the wisps responded simultaneously. "What matters is that your uncle insists you are to come to him." The wisps unsheathed glass-like longswords, the proper weapons for their seven-foot frames.

Thalia clenched the necklace and squinted as though in prayer. "Come on necklace, do your thing."

Nothing happened.

"This must be a joke," Thalia said in a panic.

The wisps slowly began closing the 10-foot gap between them and Thalia. Their swords extended, they moved closer and even closer. They appeared almost robotic to Thalia. Their faces held know expressions, neither sympathy or anger, only a rigid, dutiful glare.

Suddenly, a large lioness rammed two of the wisps. It leaped out of nowhere. The lioness was assisted by Celio, who strikes the third wisp with a wooden staff in the back of the knees.

"Leave my sister alone!" Celio said as he leaped into the fray.

"Celio!" Thalia said in shock.

"Run!" Celio said.

Thalia ran as the wisps regained their feet. The lioness sat on her haunches between the wisps and the pond, protecting Thalia as she fled. From their abdomen, the wisps ejected projectiles that nearly missed the lioness, who dodged the icy missiles as they landed at her feet. She let out a thunderous roar and stalked the ghostly wisps.

Thalia reached the edge of the pond as Celio hugged her from behind.

"Celio, get away!" Thalia pushed her brother away.

"Take me with you," Celio screamed.

"No. You must run! Quickly!" Thalia turned

to the pond.

The lioness ran towards Thalia as the icy spikes shattered at her paws. Soon the spikes were flying past Thalia as the wisps were approaching.

"Now would be a good time to depart," Twilight said. She had transformed to the lioness, only when she sensed danger. Quickly, she changed back to your ordinary cat. "Long goodbyes are over-appreciated."

"Enough!" the wisps demanded.

From their midsections, luminous tentacles protruded from the wisps with the ferocity of an arrow flying with wind. Two struck Twilight, striking her to the ground. Two more struck Celio, knocking him to the ground as well. Both were left unconscious. The other two fist-like tentacles pummelled Thalia into the water. The air in her lungs left her body, and the sky began spinning into darkness. She was left in a dreamscape as she floated beneath the waters. Her arms dangled above her thin frame, and her legs were left limp from the concussive force.

As she floated beneath its depths, she dreamed of days in the not-so-distant past:

Celio sat with his legs folded next to the Pond of Sincerity as smallmouth bass frolicked while in search of food. Next to him sat Thalia. She brushed her hair from her almond-shaped eyes.

"I do not know why, but I must go." Thalia pouted as she stared over the shiny pond. Sunlight glittered over the clear, blue waters. A slight zephyr created ripples over its surface.

Celio cried, tears trickled down both cheeks. "I do not know why I cry. I am alone with my books usually."

Thalia chuckled. "Too smart for your own good."

"It's not funny. This time you won't come back. I know it, just like Father."

"Don't say that. It's bad luck. Besides, what can happen to me. Mother says we can live forever."

"Celio looked downward at the dirt beneath him. "Last moon. do you know what happened to me?"

Thalia shook her head.

"I hit my toe on the stone over there. It hurt me." Celio looked up at Thalia with a concerned stare. "If I can hurt, we can hurt."

Thalia had almost reached the bottom. Underwater flora swayed beneath her. Before her body hit the pond floor, her body began to glow until her entire frame dissipated into a series of blinding streaks of light.

She was gone from this plane.

4.

Lost Kindness

Thalia awoke on the floor of a dimly-lit chamber. Beneath her was bedding consisting of a straw material. Torches decorated the walls, which occasionally flickered. The room was void of any furniture, only her bedding and a fire pit. Near the fire pit was a small figure tending to the logs on fire. Through her hazy vision she saw that the man was barefoot and had his hair tied in a slipknot atop his head. He appeared somewhat disheveled, and he wore a dingy *jinbei*, a pajama-like kimono with short pants and a waist-deep top. Thalia also noticed she was adorned with the same garb.

"Who...?" Thalia muttered as the Kai Stone

vibrated as she spoke. "Who are you?"

The man had an amiable smile as he turned to face Thalia. He left his kneeling position and crabbed his way to Thalia. He held what appeared to be a cup of some kind.

"I am Natto." He bowed before Thalia and raised the cup. "I made you some hot water to quench your thirst." A young man, Natto couldn't be more than 25.

Hesitantly, Thalia grabbed the stone cup and began sipping the warm liquid. She smiled slightly. "It's good. Thank you."

"You are welcome," Natto said humbly as he stared at Thalia with a look of astonishment.

Thalia gave the cup back to Natto. She slowly wiped the residual water from the corners of her lips. There was a certain dryness in her throat that she had never felt before. *Is this what they call "thirst"?*

Thalia stood and scanned her clothing, similar to the strange man before her, except hers was decorated with a flowery pattern. "Where am I?"

Natto gave her a look of confusion. "You are under the protection of the *Northern Fujiwara* clan.

A feeling of incompleteness overwhelmed Thalia. "What is Fu-ji-wawa?"

"Fujiwara," Natto corrected her as he began cleaning her feet with a wet rag. He shook his head. "You must not be from here. You are in *Mutsu Province*." He continued to scrub away at her feet. "The lord does not like dirty feet."

Thalia grabbed his arm. "You must help me." She stared into his eyes.

Natto shook nervously. "I...I..." Before he

could finish his thought, the two heard footsteps coming in the direction of the chamber's entrance. Immediately, Natto began prostrating with his forehead touching the floor.

Three men entered the room. Two were adorned in leather armor with spiked helmets, each carried a long spear. Both men guarded the doorway as the third man approached Thalia and Natto. His head was bald, and he wore a goatee that was tied at his chin with a gold-hued string. He wore a robe decorated with dragons and lions. He wore his wooden sandals, refusing to go barefoot. Although he was large in stature, his face portrayed a stoic peacefulness about him.

"I am Benkei, servant of his lord, Yoshitsune." Benkei bowed to Thalia and tugged at the cloth wrapped around his waistline. "We found you in the Snowy Mountains. Fortunate we did before the *Tengu*," Benkei said with a smile.

Natto pushed Thalia from her backside. "You must bow!"

Confused, Thalia lowered her head while looking at Benkei.

Benkei let out a hefty chuckle. "It's okay. You are unfamiliar with our customs?"

Thalia lifted her head but remained on her knees. "I am on a journey through these lands. Forgive me," Thalia said.

"Ah, journey. That is what it is called now?" Benkei stooped down to come face to face with Thalia. " Are you sure you are not a spy for the *Taira*?" Benkei's face contorted to a more serious expression.

"Who? No!" Thalia lurched forward to emphasize her sincerity. "I am not from this land."

"Where are you from?" Benkei said with a

inquisitive stare.

"I'm from...I'm from..." Thalia second-guessed her response. She estimated that her answer would not be understood. *Mother warned me that man will fear what they do not understand.*

"I am from--," Thalia said, unsure what would come next.

Natto leaped to his feet. "I believe she hails from the flatlands far to the north, a mere country bumpkin'," Natto interjected abruptly.

Thalia turned to Natto. She could not understand why this man blurted out that response. It was a good thing, however. She could not explain her true beginnings.

Benkei was taken aback and rose to his feet. "Is that so?" He gazed in Thalia's direction, what seemed like an eternity to her. "We shall see, Young Sparrow. Indeed, we shall see."

Benkei walked to the doorway. With his back facing Thalia, he said, "The lord wishes to meet the stranger. Prepare her, and have her brought to the gardens." Benkei exited the chamber, followed by the two guards.

Thalia faced Natto. Out of a small portal behind him, she noticed a beam of sunlight peaking through a crevice of the wooden window cover.

5.

Hangan

The palace's garden was flourished with colorful flowers from the Hiei Mountains. The reddish sunlight cascaded over greenery, and the humming birds feasted in the tube-like blossoms that populated the ancient pottery. It was difficult to tell where the man-made garden started and the surrounding natural forest ended. In the middle of this peaceful paradise stood Yoshitsune.

This is where the lone samurai practiced his swordplay. Every slash was effortless. Each leaf that fell from the deciduous trees overhead were sliced in half at the mercy of his *katana's* sharp edge. Once completed, Yoshitsune stood with his hands and head in a praying motion.

Yoshitsune stood about six feet tall. His long, dark hair was tied in a pony tail, and he was adorned in an aristic robe of flowers and tigers of prehistoric breed. Unlike the others she had encountered in this realm, Thalia noticed the pale skin of the young man.

Yoshitsune turned to face Thalia, who appeared more to his satisfaction. The palace's handmaidens fitted a white *kimono* on Thalia. The long dress was decorated with images of sparrows in flight. Her hair was arranged in a bun hairstyle, several flowers protruded beautifully from her ebony-hued hair-piece.

"What is your name?" Yoshitsune said with an expressionless demeanor.

"Thalia," she answered with confidence.

"You can call me Ushiwakamaru,"

Yoshitsune responded. "When I was a lad, the monks at the temple called me that."

"Lord Yosh....I mean Lord Ushiwakamaru, I'm in search of something," Thalia said without thinking.

"One can tell, you do not belong in Hiraizumi." Ushiwakamaru placed his sword within scabbard on a nearby, stone bench. "What are you searching for, Thalia?"

Thalia searched her thoughts for a moment. "A scroll," she said. "I must find it."

Ushiwakamaru moved closer to Thalia. "Is that so?" He then circled her, staring at her narrow frame. "And tell me, Thalia. What power does this scroll hold?"

"More power than you will ever know," Thalia said in a nervous tone.

Ushiwakamaru face became stern, perhaps

with a bit of obstinacy. "You are not from these lands, yet you speak our tongue." Ushiwakamaru stepped back. "At dawn, we leave for *Omi Province*. You can travel with us as my guest."

Thalia's true age revealed itself. Although she appeared 14 years old to the common on-looker, she had observed this world for five milleniums. It was a confusing perception for the curious eyes. She remembered that these lands would one day become the unified nation of Japan, a story Celio once uttered in the forest. Nonetheless, she felt lost in this fledgling time.

"Thank you, Ushiwakamaru. I choose to accompany you and your people," Thalia said without realizing the effects of her words.

Ushiwakamaru appeared puzzled. *Your people?* He immediately turned his back and stepped away from Thalia. At that moment, Benkei and two soldiers entered the garden.

"Take her to the guest chambers. She will travel with us at sun's break," Ushiwakamaru ordered to Benkei.

"Come, Little Sparrow. I will take you there," said Benkei.

Just as they were exiting the garden, Ushiwakamaru had one last departing thought for Thalia.

"Thalia, I'm not sure if you're a spy for the Taira or *Minamoto*. Just remember, I will be watching you," Ushiwakamaru said as though spoken to the air.

Thalia stopped and looked over her shoulder. She saw Ushiwakamaru staring at the ground with sword in hand. Her instincts warned her to keep her inner thoughts to herself. With that, she left the peaceful garden.

Later that evening, among the villagers and Ushiwakamaru's army, a *Noh* performance was entertaining the audience. There was laughter and clapping to the sound of thunderous drumming and plucking of several *shamisens*. Noh was a play that retold ancient tales of heroes and their journeys. Often, these stories were lacking truthfulness as long as they covered true event that occurred in the past. Alone on a makeshift stage was a geisha. However, it was a man with his face coated in white makeup and wearing a wig of some sort.

Thalia was part of the festivities. She viewed the performance with intrigue. Next to her sat Natto. They both were dressed in woolen garb to shield them from the cool winds of autumn, although a pit-fire stoked nearby to help keep them warm. They were given wooden stools to sit on, not very comfortable.

"This the Tale of the *Genji*," Natto explained to Thalia. "But, I'm sure you are familiar with the tale."

Thalia did not respond. She simply stared ahead.

"A touching tale from thousands of moons ago," Natto continued. "Hikaru must win the adoration of his true love. Not to warm his side but to capture her heart...forever."

"Forever," Thalia muttered under her breath.

"He falls for a lowly girl from the slums. As the son of an emperor, this is frowned upon," Natto said in a whisper. "So his stepmother puts a curse on his happiness."

Suddenly, another figure appeared on stage. He fell to his knees and begs the geisha to remember him if he should fall in the upcoming battle. He was covered in facial-paint as well. His cries were whiny and humorsome to the crowd. Laughter filled the audience. They began clapping to support the hero of the play.

Thalia's eyes did not deceive her. The hero was played by Ushiwakamaru. His foolish portrayal of a warrior who had fallen for the unremarkable beauty. As Ushiwakamaru begged tirelessly for her affection, the heroine blushed under a mosaic hand-fan covering her smile. That's when the audience became flustered as the cranky stepmother ran on stage and pummeled Ushiwakamaru playfully with a broom. The crowd laughed as Ushiwakamaru curled to protect his head. The stepmother wore a weathered robe and scraggly hair. Her makeup was disheveled, lipstick smeared across her cheeks.

"That's Benkei!" Thalia shouted more to

herself than those who surrounded her.

Benkei, playing the stepmother role, waved the broom in the air. "You will never know true love!"

"I am not a boy! You cannot tell me who I can love!" Ushiwakamaru said in the direction of the crowd.

"Can't I? I shall cast a spell to forbid such disobedience," Benkei shouted to the crowd.

The heroine covered Ushiwakamaru with her embrace. "You cannot!"

"Watch me!" Benkei said with an over-enthusiastic grin.

Thalia was entertained but did not quite understand why Ushiwakamaru would lower himself to participate in a ritual that makes him the butt of a joke to commoners. As the on-lookers shouted for Ushiwakamaru's character, Hikaru, to fight back. Thalia chuckled as their requests went on ignored.

Another night of slumber in which Thalia pined for her family in the other realm. She spent most of her nights daydreaming, averaging only the required one-hour sleep for her people. Their metabolism slowed to a crawl during this time, optimizing their brain activity during wake time.

Thalia remembered when she and Celio reached the Spirit of Kalas for the first time:

Thalia and Celio dug their fingers into the moist soil. Both were kneeling near the north bank of the Pond of Sincerity. Thalia looked up and saw her parents looking on, as well as her uncle, Enlil. They were dressed in robed garb, traditional dress of the Marlet Kingdom. They looked on with intrigue. However, Thalia could not decipher her father's face. His face appeared as only a shadow. Thalia could not remember what Nuru looked like. It had been so long.

Thalia and Celio recanted the ancient language of their people, a language that was guttural in sound. As they spoke, the soil rose up their arms, penetrating their very skin until it covered their entire body. They both gasped for air, wondering if it was their last breath.

The coolness of the night air soon overcame Thalia. She drifted off into a deep sleep.

6.

Tengu Tales

Ushiwakamaru led his caravan of armored samurai on horseback and spear-wielding foot soldiers through the Hiei Mountains. Leaves began to fall with autumn in full steam. The clouds overhead blocked the sunlight, creating a dim, eerie essence across the landscape.

Ushiwakamaru was dressed in full armor. He wore a large *kabuto* on his head. Two golden horn-like rods protruded from its pate and the cheek-guards were decorated with tigers in stalking mode. As the horses slowly galloped along, he turned to his most loyal retainer, Benkei, riding along side of him.

"The tengu are said to strike only at night," Ushiwakamaru said plainly.

Benkei wiped his bald head and brow of the day's sweat. "The priests at Kurama has given us protection from the sneaky demons, my lord."

"It will be days before we reach my brother in Omi Province," Ushiwakamaru added while surveying the path before him.

Benkei tilted his head in indecision. "Forgive, my lord. I would never question your actions."

Ushiwakamaru smiled and removed his heavy helmet. "That would be a first. What do you want to say, Benkei?"

'Well, my lord, can we trust Yoritomo to honor the alliance? I know he is your brother, but it has been a long time."

"He is of the Minamoto as I am. Yes, I trust

him,' Ushiwakamaru said as he nodded to reassure himself.

"So is Yoshinaka, your cousin," Benkei said with one brow arched. He repositioned his leather armor to fit around his neck.

Ushiwakamaru pretended to ignore his friend and servant. He stroked the mane of his horse gently and then patted it, pleased by the endurance of the great beast.

"What do you think of the girl?" Ushiwakamaru said.

"The foreigner, my lord?" Benkei answered.

Ushiwakamaru nodded with an approving grunt.

"Last night, I instructed two of my men to remove the necklace she wears. While she slept, they tried. Both men suffered burns that can only be sent by the gods. Their hands have a mark in a language unknown to every priest I showed... We should kill her now, my lord. She is a witch, not to be trusted. How do we know she was not sent by the Taira?" Benkei said with stifled emotion.

"Is that so?" Ushiwakamaru gazed forward as his white horse trotted along. "We'll continue until sundown and make camp at the base of the mountains."

Benkei was puzzled that Ushiwakamaru had not responded to his perception of Thalia but bowed his head immediately. "As you wish, my lord."

Before Benkei rode away and delivered Ushiwakamaru's orders to the rest of the men, Ushiwakamaru had a parting thought.

"Benkei, Lord Hidehira taught me many things as a child after my father was killed. He taught me that witches come in two types of varieties, the bad and the good." Ushiwakamaru gazed at the sky as the sunlight peaked through the clouds. He whispered to himself, "Which is she?"

Thalia and Natto rode in a wagon several yards behind Ushiwakamaru. The wooden wagon was filled with hay and smelled of cow dung, most likely those that trailed behind the caravan.

Thalia chewed on a piece of dried meat, unsure of its species. She was new to the tough, salty flesh. Her eyes squinted with each bite, unfulfilled by its flavor. Natto, on the other hand, ate his portion in a cheerful manner.

"We will camp tonight, I hear," Natto explained to Thalia seated next to him. "There will be plenty to refreshing water along the mouth of the stream...unless the tengu are guarding it tonight."

"The who?" Thalia said.

"The tengu are the demons of the forest. Some say they are fallen warriors from past battles." Natto finished his dried meat and belched to digest its contents.

Thalia took another bite and looked ahead. "Tell me about your lord. Does he have a wife?"

"From what I can tell, he only values the Minamoto Clan. That is his family. Growing up on the run must have been difficult."

"One cannot tell," Thalia said with concern.

"Yes, Lord Yoritomo and Lord Yoshitsune had to go into hiding since their father's and brother's death. The rebellion cost the family dearly. The remaining brothers scattered until now."

Thalia threw the remaining dried meat from her hand. "What about your family? Where are they?"

Natto looked away. "They are far away. They betrayed me, so now I must make my own name." Natto stood in the wagon, which was slowing. "It looks like we'll be camping soon," Natto said abruptly.

Thalia could see the sun going down in the distance. The horizon of mountains had a crimson hue and gave way to a river of crystal-blue waters that penetrated the dim forest ahead.

Later that night, Thalia stared at the starry night sky as shooting stars danced across the clear heavens. Sleep came early tonight. The camp had already had repast, and the soldiers were bedded for the night, except for the camp guards patrolling for unseen dangers.

Natto awoke to the glow illuminating from Thalia's neck, who was sound asleep, or so he thought. The necklace glowed brighter as Thalia sat up with her eyes still shut.

"Thalia?" Natto whispered.

She stood up as though she never heard him. She walked aimlessly towards the forest surrounding them.

"Thalia, no!" Natto screamed silently as Thalia disappeared into the darkness of the sinister forest.

7.

They Know

Thalia stood in the middle of a clearing, now with her eyes wide open. Only the moonlight gave her enough vision to see the shadows lurking in the surrounding forest. Thalia could feel a chill overcome her very being as the tengu entered the clearing. They numbered 30 or so to her count.

The tengu were grotesque from head to toe. They stood about five-foot tall and were pale as though they were wearing muddy, white masks. Their golden-like pupils were outlined in black ink. Horns protruded from their foreheads and blood filled their mouths, coating their vampire-like fangs.

"We know who you are, little girl," one tengu man or woman (hard to distinguish) said. "We are familiar with your world."

"I do not fear you," Thalia said as her lips trembled.

"You should be afraid," another tengu said. He moved closer to Thalia. His three-inch claws waved inches from her face. "You should be very much afraid, for we eat people and spit out their bones like the fleshy worms they are inclined."

"You hide in darkness, fearful of my father's light." Thalia chuckled as she extended her index finger. "You call yourselves warriors? I only see monsters who want nothing but hurt and sympathy."

Suddenly, the tengu all let out a deafening shriek that caused Thalia to shake momentarily. They all showed themselves by stepping into the moonlight. Their backs were hunched over as the hair on their backs became stiff like a cat on the prowl.

"You speak bravely for someone of your age," another tengu said. This one wore a velvet cape with human jawbones attached to it. "Chark would rip your spine from your head, normally. However, we will make haste with your demise since you are a brave girl."

Thalia clenched her fists as the tengu surrounded her and moved closer, grunting similar to a pack of ghouls looking to feast.

"Back!" Thalia raised her fist and began to glow from head to toe.

"First, we're going to eat you and then the army that rode with you!" Chark said as his claws extended to a horrific eight inches.

Thalia eyes were pupil-less, and her

eyebrows arched, giving her a formidable appearance. "Get back!" The Necklace of Daichi ejected beams of light, and the Vulcan Stone released a concussive force with the power of tornado winds. The tengu flew back on their rears and cried like startled hyenas.

"I do not want to fight, but the stones brought me here." Thalia's voice was deep, and her opaque stare sent a intimidating presence their direction. The timid tengu fell to their knees in fear of the little girl.

"Forgive us, little girl. We did not mean to offend you," Chark said as he bowed before Thalia.

"I'm not a little girl," Thalia said without hesitation.

"Yes, you're right, Thalia," another tengu added. "Perhaps, we can offer you a trinket as tribute to your power?"

"How did you know my name?" Thalia said as her eyes returned to normal, and the glowing ceased.

"We all know who you are and why you are here, Thalia," Chark interceded. "You are the daughter of Gaia, goddess of fallen warriors."

"So why did you try to scare me?" Thalia looked dumbfounded.

The tengu stood up and looked at one another. They raised their palms in confusion.

"That's what we do," Chark said as if it was the obvious response.

"Horrible," Thalia said with a disgusted snarl.

"You're searching for the scroll," Chark said as if to change the subject.

"Yes. Where can I find it?" Thalia was eager

to know.

Chark thought to himself and smiled with self-satisfaction. "You seek the Scroll of Purity. That is what you seek."

"Where can I find it?" Thalia said.

"It is here, where you least suspect it," Chark answered. "I could show you, but it would burn me alive. That would hurt a deal greatly since I am already dead."

"Well then, just tell me where it is," Thalia said after a long sigh.

"It is in the hearts of mankind," Chark said. "Only those of the purist heart can abstract what is something that cannot be possessed or held." Chark wiped saliva from the edge of his mouth.

"That is very helpful. Thank you," Thalia said, satisfied with the information. "I will search these lands."

Chark raised an index finger to his lips and tilted his head to one side. "As gratitude, can we still devour your friends in the army?"

"No!" Thalia quickly said.

"Curses. Oh well, maybe next time. What a feast they would have been," Chark said disappointedly. "We must go now."

Thalia stared at the tengu as they all blended into the forest backdrop, their pale faces disappeared into the landscape.

Just as they departed, Benkei and several foot soldiers ran up with swords drawn. Benkei carried his customary halbert. Benkei espied the scene and faced Thalia.

"What happened?" Benkei wondered. "I heard you scream. Why the hell are you out here? The tengu are known to roam these forests."

Thalia stared him directly in the eye. "They

were helping me find the scroll. Now I know where to look."

Benkei exhaled with frustration and stepped away shaking his head. "Are you kidding me? I knew I should have killed you the first time I saw you. You are a strange girl, Young Sparrow."

At the same time, Natto approached Thalia. He scratched his head and placed his hands on his hips. "Never mind him. I think he likes you."

Thalia gazed up to the moon, wondering if she would succeed or fail.

8.

Brothers Remember

As Ushiwakamaru's forces marched into the dusty village in Omi Province, the villagers lined the warriors' path in a bowing position. The village was small, relative to the massive castle-towns found in the larger provinces. It was a farming community, rice being their largest crop. However, cows littered the fields of the scenic topography. Children offered the newcomers with flowers picked from the local flora. Heavy drums echoed to welcome Ushiwakamaru and his army.

Ushiwakamaru rode in with Benkei riding at his side. He was dressed in his wartime kimono, a leather, embroidered substitute for full plate armor.

A large cap rested on his head, black and simple in design.

"The tengu caused no problems during the night," Ushiwakamaru said to Benkei in a monotone manner.

Benkei shrugged and laughed boisterously. "Perhaps they feared the power of the Minamoto!" He said it in jest but could not comprehend the passiveness of the tengu.

"I am to greet my brother at the capitol. Make sure the men are rested and fed. We battle in two nights," Ushiwakamaru shared with his close friend and lead retainer.

"As you wish, my lord," Benkei answered. Then he offered with hesitation, "What of the girl?"

"Which girl do you speak of?" Ushiwakamaru said.

"The young sparrow, the foreigner, my lord," Benkei said in obvious fashion.

"Keep a watchful eye on her," Ushiwakamaru said. "Still I wonder what and why the ancestors have presented her to me."

Later that day, Ushiwakamaru sat crosslegged in a room with little decor, except for the burning torches and artistic painting that lined the walls. Before him was a single pillow on the floor.

In walked Yoritomo and his entourage, a group of aging men in kimonos. As Yoritomo took a seat on the pillow, the men sat near Ushiwakamaru. They all bowed before Yoritomo, who gazed at them as one does a patch of lilies.

Yoritomo had a slender build and stood about five-and-a-half feet tall. He was dressed in a white-and-gold kimono with tigers embroidered on the fabric. He stroked his goatee and smiled at his brother before him.

Ushiwakamaru raised his head and planted his fist on the floor. "It is good to see you in great health, Yoritomo."

Yoritomo paused for a moment, nodding in agreement. He stood and walked to Ushiwakamaru. He stared closely at the warrior-lad, impressed by how much he had grown since childhood.

"Rise, Ushiwakamaru," Yoritomo said as he extended his arms. "It has been too long, Brother."

Ushiwakamaru stood. His eyesight met Yoritomo's. "Yoritomo, my army and I are at your command."

Yoritomo caressed Ushiwakamaru's shoulders and shook him gently. "Ignore the formalities Ushiwakamaru. I thought I would never see you again. This makes me very pleased."

Ushiwakamaru smiled and his eyes sparkled with joy. They had not seen each other since they were boys, since Yoritomo and his other brothers were banished to Izu Province.

"The Taira will pay for what they did to father and our brothers," Yoritomo said with conviction. "Prince Mochito has given us free reign to recapture the lands. It will be joyous."

Ushiwakamaru lowered his head. "Mother has passed. She died peacefully in her bed," Ushiwakamaru said in sadness.

Yoritomo looked away. "I heard she lived a fine life, regardless of-"

"We must avenge her grief," Ushiwakamaru said abruptly. "We owe her that much."

"We will. We will," Yoritomo said as he

nodded to his brother.

Yoritomo returned to sitting on the pillow. Ushiwakamaru sat. He folded his arms within the cloth of his bulky kimono.

"How many men do you have?" Yoritomo got straight to the point.

"One thousand, but they fight with the strength of ten thousand."

"That is good. The men must need rest from their journey." Yoritomo waved his hand, and a woman carrying a tray of two bowls scurried to deliver the bowls to both men.

"Thank you, Brother." Ushiwakamaru bowed and sipped the warm bowl of water. Yoritomo did the same.

Thalia and Celio approached the large boulder within the dark, damp cave. The rock that covered their bodies flickered away, leaving their forms. They could only hear the drips of water seeping through the crevices of their surroundings.

Celio paused in his tracks at the large boulder before them. "I'm afraid."

Thalia turned to Celio. "So am I." She then placed her palms on the giant stone. Celio followed soon after. The giant boulder began glowing violet but remained cold to the touch.

Thalia felt an energy overwhelm her, but it did not hurt in a physical way. Tears began rolling down her cheeks. The pain she felt was unlike that felt before this test. Thousands of years of memories streaked through her body, unforgiving to her young, fragile psyche. It was the Spirit of Kalas, the power one can never comprehend.

It was the afternoon before battle. The men

were practicing their melee techniques in the camp. Officers were training new recruits for possible glory. Boys were practicing the spear, in hope of fighting for their lord. The sun beat down relentlessly on all that day.

Not far away, Thalia and Natto picked rice from the paddies. Their ankles were covered in dirty water and muddy soil. The stench of earth brought back memories of home for Thalia.

"I will never understand humans desire to wage war over ground that belongs to everyone," Thalia said in disgust.

"Of course not, you are a girl. You don't understand men," Natto said as he plucked the plant from the soil. He chuckled. "Still, you are human as well."

"I try to be," Thalia said under her breath.

"What was that?"

"Nothing."

Thalia caught Natto by surprise and started staring over his shoulder. He followed the direction of her vision and found Yoritomo in the distance aiming his bow. A party of a few men silently cheered their lord on.

"It's Lord Yoritomo. I hear he likes to sharpen his skills in a hunt before every battle," Natto said matter-of-factly. "Usually he hunts squirrels and rabbits."

Thalia dropped her basket. "What do squirrels and rabbits do to him?"

"Nothing, I suppose. Haven't you eaten them before?"

"No." Determined, Thalia started walking towards Yoritomo and his men.

Natto dropped his basket and ran to catch up with Thalia. "Are you insane?" Natto shouted, hoping to instill fear in the girl. "You cannot question a lord."

Thalia pushed him away and gained her footing on more solid ground. Barefoot, with her tunic soaking wet from sweat, she marched on, ignoring the servant's words.

"He can't kill my creatures with impunity," Thalia said without hesitation.

Yoritomo enjoyed hunting before every battle. It calmed his nerves. There is not much larger game in this province, but he made do. With his leather arm protector on, he cocked his bow and aimed the arrow at an unsuspecting grey squirrel atop a nearby tree.

"Good luck, my lord," said one of his retainers.

Everyone was quiet as Yoritomo steadied his focus. The squirrel was still in his line of sight. He took two deep breaths, and just as he let go of the arrow-

"Stop!" Thalia threw his shot off, purposely.

The arrow flew by its target, and the squirrel scurried away into the convenient hole in the tree. Yoritomo spun around in a rage. He stared at Thalia with the intensity of a tsunami wave.

"You fool! I had him!"

Immediately, all the men with Yoritomo drew their blades. Thalia stepped back in shock. Yoritomo threw his prized bow to the ground.

"You can't harm a defenseless animal. That is a living creature!" Thalia said while taking a deep swallow.

"Who in the *Hachiman* are you?" Yoritomo screamed at Thalia. "I want to know who I am killing today!"

"You can't harm a defenseless creature, no

more than you can harm another being," Thalia said with a tightened jaw.

"Is that so?" Yoritomo said with a joking overtone.

Thalia nodded in confidence. Hunting was forbidden in her land. Gaia would never allow it.

Natto ran up and fell to his knees. "Forgive her, my lord! She is not from here!"

Yoritomo's henchmen surrounded him with swords drawn. They stared at the girl with great discontent. *How dare you insult our lord?*

Yoritomo drew his bow and aimed an arrow directly at Thalia. "You are a malcontent, little girl."

Thalia stood there and did not flinch. She stood strong in her belief. Expecting the Necklace of Daichi to react, she squinted, waiting for its power to unleash upon her assailants.

The men, including Natto, froze in Thalia's view. They gasped at her very presence, or so she thought. The men shivered and fled, except Yoritomo and Natto. The two men stood there in awe of Thalia's uncompromising stance, or so she thought.

"Thalia, watch out!" Natto launched himself in Thalia's direction.

Thalia was confused. *Did they not see the power of the necklace?* She tilted her little brown head and looked down at the necklace. It was not glowing. "What are they afraid of?" Thalia thought, perplexed by the men's sudden dash of fear. That was until she heard the roar behind her.

Right behind Thalia stood a 12-foot black bear with its claws extended to pounce. Her jaw dropped in surprise. Natto immediately pushed her out of range of danger. Thalia fell to the ground.

The dust kicked up, causing her to cough profusely.

RARGH!

The bear knocked Natto to the ground with a single swipe. Streaks of blood appeared on the little man's forehead. Dazed from the blow, he let out a subtle scream.

Yoritomo let loose a single arrow. The projectile simply struck the bear in the abdomen, which the beast broke away as though scratching a mosquito bite. If anything, it made the bear even more enraged. The bear ignored Thalia completely and ran towards Yoritomo with unyielding certainty.

"Ahhh!" Yoritomo fell on his butt, trying to load another arrow to defend himself.

Suddenly, the bear stopped in its tracks. It turned in the direction of Thalia, breathing heavy from the fierce action.

Thalia stood there with her arms extended. The Kai Stone on the necklace glowed, causing the earth beneath Thalia to glow violet as well.

The bear approached Thalia slowly, carefully sniffing at every step. His giant nostril snuggled into Thalia's chest, calming the beast.

Thalia placed a gentle palm on the bear's head, slowly rubbing it like a pet. The beast had calmed down with her loving touch.

"Nothing to worry about, girl. You don't have to protect me," Thalia whispered to the bear.

Natto and Yoritomo looked on in total shock. Yoritomo lowered his bow as the bear dashed away deep into the forest. Thalia's necklace ceased to glow. She walked over to Natto and grabbed his hand.

"Thank you, friend."

Natto nodded quickly and smiled with gratitude. "I'll always be by you side."

"Hey!" Yoritomo was not pleased. In fact he was pissed off. He slammed his bow to the ground. "I am unsure of what I just saw, but that still does not give you a pass for interrupting my hunt."

"Surely, my lord, she just saved our lives," Natto said to quickly defend Thalia. "Couldn't you forgive her for this one time?"

Yoritomo sighed as he stared at Thalia, who bore a look of a disciplined puppy. "Never say that Yoritomo is not a man of mercy."

The wooden-piked door slammed shut in Thalia's face, rattling the outdoor cage she was entrapped. "This is your idea of mercy," Thalia screamed at the guard walking away. The sun set in the distance, giving way to darkness.

9.

Blood Deep

Thalia absorbed the pain, the celebrations and the strife felt by those over hundreds of generations. She knew it was a test of her will to endure what others felt. The emotions hit her like a tidal wave. Celio did not fare better. She watched as her brother was brought to his knees by the power of the stone. Yet, they both kept their palms on the boulder.

Thalia witnessed the betrayal of mankind. She saw many falling under the sword of their brothers and fathers. The feeling of loss was relentless until it stopped. There was silence of the uncanny type. Reality had left the cave, only her thoughts guided her. Tears rolled down Thalia's cheeks. She closed her eyes, hoping it would go away like waking from a bad dream. When she opened them, she was at another place. It was an open field with the earth covered in lilies. The sun beamed down heavy on her shoulders.

Gaia stood behind her, towering over Thalia's shivering frame. Gaia caressed Thalia's shoulders and whispered softly into her ear.

"You must let the fear go before it controls you. Understand the feelings that surround you."

"Should I be afraid?" Thalia said cautiously.

Gaia stepped back and narrowed her eyes at Thalia. She gritted her teeth and spread her arms apart. "Your most fears dwell within you, daughter. Rejoice in them."

"What if I-?"

Gaia's eyes glowed, and Thalia's entire body burst into flames. Thalia screamed in agonizing pain.

Natto was first to greet Thalia in the morning. She lifted herself from the floor of the makeshift holding cell. She slept longer each day as though she was conforming to her surroundings.

"They can't keep you here for long," Natto said as he slid a bowl of rice between the wooden bars. "Lord Yoshitsune will not stand for it."

Thalia closed her eyes and re-opened them with a big smile. "You know, I could get out of here if I wanted to leave."

Natto laughed as he grabbed his abdomen. He waved his hand in the air to help settle himself. "Get out of here! Why, you're but a little girl!" He continued to laugh boisterously until he saw Thalia not laughing. To the contrary, she stared him down with a stern glare. It was as though she stared through him. A cold chill overcame his very essence.

Thalia broke the silence. "I have to find the scroll. Staying here does not help that."

"I will help you. Like I said, I will never leave your side." Natto smiled and let his fingers stroke the wooden bars.

"Hurry, Natto, for it is fast approaching," Thalia said as though speaking to the sky above.

"What do you mean? What is coming?" Natto said.

Thalia's vision turned to the blazing sun beaming down between the grey clouds. "Unforeseen betrayal."

"What can I do?" Ushiwakamaru paced the

floor of the large room reserved for him in the castle.

"You are responsible for her, my lord," Benkei said while sitting with his legs crossed.

"Where is she now?" Ushiwakamaru said with a sigh in disgust.

"Lord Yoritomo has her kept in the cells outside the castle walls."

Ushiwakamaru sat on the tatami mat across from Benkei. He folded his arms underneath his silk kimono. Ushiwakamaru grunted from a sharp pain that shot through his right shoulder.

"Are you okay, my lord?" Benkei said as he extended a hand with concern.

"Yes, Benkei," Ushiwakamaru said as he dismissed his friend's worrisome stare. "An arrow found me in the last battle. Nothing to lose heart over."

Exasperated, Benkei snarled at his long-time friend. He cared for Ushiwakamaru since he was a child and faced many battles together. "Your mind must had been somewhere else to be so careless."

"What do you mean?" Ushiwakamaru defended his honor without hesitation.

"Perhaps she would make a fine wife. It's time."

Ushiwakamaru stood up in defiance of Benkei's remark. "What? She's but a child."

"Not much younger than my lord." Benkei smirked. "Your eyes do not seem to think so."

Ushiwakamaru laughed. "That's your problem, Benkei. You see what is not there."

"If you say so, my lord," Benkei said with a slight chuckle.

Ushiwakamaru walked to the open portal that let in a beam of sunlight. He squinted as the glare irritated his eyes. "Does she know?"

Benkei shook his head. "My men spoke to no other, my lord."

Ushiwakamaru lowered his head in contemplation. "Good." He looked in Benkei's direction. "This is a test from the gods. Why do I care for this child? It is as though Thalia was sent here for some reason."

Natto was on his knees outside the bars that held Thalia. His bony fingers were trying to catch a grasshopper hopping across the dirt floor.

Thalia sat in the cell, staring to the sky. "Help me, Father. What am I suppose to do?" She picked up a stone and tossed it across the floor, mostly out of boredom. "Natto, I have to tell you something. I--."

Heavy footsteps approached the secure

chamber. Thalia and Natto looked up to see Ushiwakamaru and a few guards staring at them. His stoic gaze unnerved Thalia. "Guards, open this door." Ushiwakamaru looked directly at Thalia. "Come with me. I have something to show you."

Ushiwakamaru and Thalia stepped into the airy chamber reserved for Ushiwakamaru. The guards remained at the door. Thalia's eyes widened in complete surprise and joy.

"Celio!" Thalia said as she sprinted to embrace her brother standing in the chamber. "How did you get here?"

Celio returned the hug with a big smile. He held tight to his long-lost sister. He was dressed in the tunic he wore in their home kingdom of Marlet.

"I missed you, Sister," Celio said as tears rolled down his cheeks. "You left me."

"I did not want to." Thalia was happy to see her brother, although she became concerned knowing that her little brother was no longer safe with Gaia. "You should not be here."

Ushiwakamaru let out a little smile and returned to his stoic facial expression. "We found him hiding in the forest outside the castle grounds. He speaks another language. We understood the word 'Thalia' only. Who is this?"

"He's my brother. Thank you for finding him, Ushiwakamaru." Thalia stared at Ushiwakamaru with soft eyes. A single tear trickled down her cheek.

Ushiwakamaru looked uncomfortable and blushed from the recognition. "Thank Benkei. Fortunately he found him before my brother did."

Thalia stroked the pate of Celio's head. "How did you get here? You must go back."

"When you fled, I followed you." Celio told his side.

The wisps slowly began closing the 10-foot gap between them and Thalia. Their swords extended, they moved closer and even closer. They appeared almost robotic to Thalia. Their faces held no expressions, neither sympathy or anger, only a rigid, dutiful glare.

Suddenly, a large lioness rammed two of the wisps. It leaped out of nowhere. The lioness was assisted by Celio, who struck the third wisp with a wooden staff in the back of the knees.

"Leave my sister alone!" Celio said as he leaped into the fray.

"Celio!" Thalia said in shock.

"Run!" Celio said.

Thalia ran as the wisps regained their feet.

The lioness sat on her haunches between the wisps and the pond, protecting Thalia as she fled. From their abdomen, the wisps ejected projectiles that nearly missed the lioness, who dodged the icy missiles as they landed at her feet. She let out a thunderous roar and stalked the ghostly wisps.

Thalia reached the edge of the pond as Celio hugged her from behind.

"Celio, get away!" Thalia pushed her brother away.

"Take me with you," Celio screamed.

"No. You must run! Quickly!" Thalia turned to the pond.

The lioness ran towards Thalia as the icy spikes shattered at her paws. Soon the spikes were flying past Thalia and the wisps were approaching.

"Now would be a good time to depart," Twilight said. She had transformed to the lioness,

only when she sensed danger. Quickly, she changed back to your ordinary cat. "Long goodbyes are over-appreciated."

"Enough!" the wisps demanded.

From their midsections, luminous tentacles protruded from the wisps with the ferocity of an arrow flying with wind. Two struck Twilight, striking her to the ground. Two more struck Celio, knocking him to the ground as well. Both were left unconscious. The other two fist-like tentacles pummelled Thalia into the water. The air in her lungs left her body, and the sky began spinning into darkness. She was left in a dreamscape as she floated beneath the waters. Her arms dangled above her thin frame, and her legs were left limp from the concussive force.

"When you disappeared under the water,

Twilight and I jumped in as well, which is a difficult feat since Twilight hates water as you know," Celio said as an afterthought.

"Where is Twilight?" Thalia said.

Celio shook his head repeatedly. "I don't know. We were separated in the lights of that weird tunnel."

Ushiwakamaru did not understand the foreign language shared by the two. He looked on in astonishment. The strangeness he felt from Thalia was only amplified. "Come, there is someone else you must meet."

Ushiwakamaru, Thalia, Benkei, Natto, and Celio prostrated themselves as Yoritomo walked into the torch-lit chamber with his retainers behind him. He had a look of disgust as he stopped abruptly at the sight of Celio. "What? There's another!" He asked in surprise.

Ushiwakamaru raised his head with his fists planted in the mat under him. "Yes, this is Celio, Thalia's brother."

Yoritomo sat cross-legged. Suddenly, he whipped out a sandalwood hand fan and waved it jerkingly across his brow. The autumn heat had caused him to perspire profusely. "Celio, a strange name for such a boy."

"You have no right to hold me prisoner. I did nothing wrong," Thalia said with bite, partly because she wanted to divert attention away from Celio.

Yoritomo stood immediately. His chest heaved up and down under his silk, black kimono. He held tightly to his fan. "You are correct. Perhaps, I should just kill you dead."

"For what crime? She saved your life, older

brother," Ushiwakamaru screamed. "You should be grateful."

Yoritomo grunted and sat cross-legged once again. This time, he waved his fan even faster. "I forgive your impertinence only because we lost our blood cousin today."

"Lord Yoritomo, do you not disagree?" Benkei interjected on Thalia's behalf. "Surely, that bear would have mauled you."

"Is it customary for your retainers to show such disrespect, Ushiwakamaru?" Yoritomo shouted.

Ushiwakamaru gazed upward with a slight smirk. "Thalia deserves the benefit of the doubt, brother."

Yoritomo slammed his fan on the tatami floor and placed his hands on his hips. "She is your problem, Ushiwakamaru. Keep her in her place or

I will."

Ushiwakamaru turned to Thalia and nodded to the stoic girl's face, she knelt there without as much as looking away from Yoritomo. Her eyes were focused on Yoritomo. It was as though she was in a trance. Thalia gritted her teeth in frustration. She wanted to blurt it out but couldn't.

"Thalia, you are free with Lord Yoritomo's blessing," Benkei said under his breath. " Take it before he changes his mind."

Celio looked up at Thalia. He could not understand their language. He could not trust himself. The prickly-haired boy from another dimension trusted his older sister only. His eyes said as much.

Thalia stood to the surprise of the rest in the room. It was disrespectful to rise above the samurai lord. "Will you not tell him? He deserves to know."

Yoritomo eyes widened. He looked at Thalia with great discontent. Somehow, he knew. She told him in his thoughts. He stood there and took a deep swallow. He extended his hand with his long, bony fingers out as a retainer brought him his longsword. Yoritomo unsheathed the blade from its scabbard. The metal sparkled from the glare of the sunlight peaking through an open portal.

Ushiwakamaru rose to his feet quickly and stood between Yoritomo and Thalia. She did not flinch but kept her gaze on the angry warlord, Yoritomo.

"You would kill a little girl?" Ushiwakamaru barked in defense of the age-deceiving girl from the Marlet Kingdom.

"She is a witch. This is not a little girl. Stand aside, Ushiwakamaru!" Yoritomo pushed the smaller of the two warriors to the floor and raised his katana for a downward strike of Thalia.

Celio dashed to Thalia and embraced his sister to protect her from the blow. Yoritomo's blade was met by Natto's forearm. The sword made a thud as it dug into Natto's flesh. Natto did not scream or cry in pain. He bowed his head before Yoritomo and rested on one knee.

"Natto!" Thalia knelt beside her friend as crimson blood trickled down his arm.

Natto panted and winced as he removed the blade. "My lord, your blade is in need of sharpening."

Thalia stood and launched herself at Yoritomo. Her fists were clenched at her side. For once, anger had overtaken her, a feeling she had never experienced. "I won't let you hurt my friends!"

Ushiwakamaru picked himself off the floor and grabbed Thalia. "No, Thalia!" He pulled her closer and took a deep breath. "He is my brother."

Their eyes met. It was as though she pleaded to Ushiwakamaru without uttering a word. *You don't understand. He--.*

At that moment, a guard in Yoritomo's army burst in and fell to his knees. "My lord, the Taira are moving against us!"

10.

Battle of Ichi-no-Tani

"You will fail me. You will fail your people!"
Gaia said as she stood above Thalia curled up on
the grassy field, smoke vapors escaped her singed
5' 4" frame.

Thalia stood in defiance. With one swipe of
her hand, the earth rose and engulfed Gaia. The
soil travelled down her throat, suffocating the
voluptuous beauty. "You are not my mother!"

The earth swallowed Gaia or what appeared
to be Thalia's mother. Sunlight changed to
moonlight, and the sounds of birds screeching
filled the dark, forbidding area. Thalia's chest
heaved up and down. Her eyes glowed as she

espied her surroundings. Darkness prevented her from seeing four feet in front of her. The air felt cold and unforgiving.

"Of course not, I am you!"

Suddenly, in a flash out of the darkness, Thalia was struck by Gaia's body, as though a strong gust of wind swept her off her feet. The force sucked the wind from her very soul. She gasped for air, grabbing her throat in a panic.

"You will always be a disappointment!" Gaia's voice trailed behind her.

"How many are there?" Yoritomo said from his mounted horse with his hand on his hilt.

"At least seven thousand men occupy all the castles." Benkei said from his saddle.

On the outskirts of the Fukuwara area of Settsu Province, the Minamoto army of 20 thousand samurai lined the open field of the mountainous region. The sound of horses neighing created a tense atmosphere in the blue skies above. The bitter cold of the autumn air made Ushiwakamaru shiver.

"A direct assault would be futile. The Taira moved on the castles before we were ready," Ushiwakamaru said with his mouth contorted.

Yoritomo held tight to his stallion's reins. "We have enough siege weapons to outlast Kiyomori. They are pinned in."

"Yes, like a spider in its web," Ushiwakamaru said abruptly as his horse trotted away from the group, followed by Benkei and his retainers.

"Where are you going?" Yoritomo shouted.

Ushiwakamaru shouted without looking back, "I have a plan."

Thalia sat alongside Natto as several female healers tended to his wounded arm. They changed the blood-soaked bandages with fresh ones. Natto appeared to be in a haze, absent from his peaceful surroundings. Thalia caressed his brow and wiped the perspiration from his pale cheeks. The serene handmaidens carried on with their duties of warm water to the deep cut and his thirst. Night was upon them.

"You fool, I can take a blow from his sword, but you cannot," Thalia said playfully as a tear streamed down her face. "You are not here in this world to protect me."

At that moment, Natto opened his eyes, awakened from his slumber. "Thalia, you're here," Natto whispered. "I told you before, I will never leave your side." Once again, he drifted back to sleep with a giant grin on his face.

Celio scampered into the tatami-floored room and knelt beside his sister. With care, Celio espied the room to insure no one could here him speak in their native tongue.

"Strange man," Celio commented with a certain curiosity. "He doesn't appear in any of my books."

A beam of moonlight pierced the small, open window, causing Thalia's ivory kimono to have a subtle glow. The torches lining the walls flickered from a slight breeze. Celio stood. His miniature frame barely fit into the oversized robe. With a few swipes of his hands in the air, once the handmaidens left the chamber, several hieroglyphs floated before him, the written language of their people.

"There is to be a great battle. The human

Ushiwakamaru will attack tonight though," Celio said as his gaze followed the floating script. "He will win the battle but at great loss. The moon will expose him."

"Many will die?" Thalia stood with steadfast concern.

Celio nodded. "Let's go home."

"Stay here and watch over Natto," Thalia said.

Gaia let the mud bath cover her from face to toe. This is where she recharged her essence, where she became one with the earth. As she soaked in the dark, muddy pool in the airy cave, the sound of moisture dripped with a human-like heartbeat. Her thoughts overcame Gaia's being, and for a brief moment, they took her back to a frightening millennium.

"You can't possibly defend them or their senseless actions," Enlil said as he smashed his fist on the porcelain table in the middle of the dark, nondescript chamber.

In the room sat a younger Gaia and Enlil alone at each end of the table. Both were dressed in traditional Anunnaki robes, the garb of the elders. On the table were several pillar-like stones that each casted a long, shadowy figure on the stone walls. It was dull and dark, with the exception of a glowing firepit.

"Enlil, you say that as though you're their judge," Gaia replied in a monotone manner. "They are not here for you to rule."

"Your affection for the Sumerians compares to the affection of that rock," Enlil said as he waves his hand and gestures to a stone on the

floor. "Do you ever tire, Gaia? Sister?"

The shadowy figures had bellowing voices of both the male and female variety, or one would hope. They took their turns to provide their take on the matter.

"We sent your tribe to make this world our own."

"Gaia, we have given you many chances."

"Chances squandered."

"Yes, indeed."

"We should have annihilated the Sumerians from the very beginning," Enlil said as he stroked his brow.

Gaia stood from her chair. She espied the room. "The 'humans' have simply lost their way. They can be saved. I will enlist my-"

"Saved?" Enlil said abruptly. He leaned back in his seat with a certain smugness that only

he could present. "By the Spirit of Kalas, leave them be, the Sumerians will destroy themselves. I just want to help them along."

"As I was explaining to the all-powerful Izkal, I will send my daughter in my place," Gaia said in a sharp tone. "She will gather the scrolls of their ancient past and return them to me."

"I hope so for your sake, Gaia."

"Do not follow the same mistakes made by Nuru."

"Yes, he may never earn his keep in the Marlet Kingdom again. Such a fool."

"Because he believed in something better?" Gaia shouted in anger. "Because he believed in what he was doing?"

"Yes, that would be exactly right," Enlil said with a small chuckle.

"The girl is ready. She will succeed before it

is too late," Gaia said with the confidence that only a mother could exude.

Enlil sighed then rose from his chair. "Thalia will never succeed. You see, Thalia lacks something every young girl needs," Enlil said as he began departing the damp chamber. "The sane guidance of a father's adoration."

"Enlil, can't you see this is the way for the Anunnaki survival here on this world?" Gaia said thoughtfully.

Enlil stopped and turned to Gaia. "It is a shame, my sister. I will stop her." Enlil then left the room.

As the flames of the firepit dimmed, Gaia knew at that moment, she would have to battle her brother.

11.

Heal Me

Ushiwakamaru, Benkei and his face-painted samurai warriors were prone in the grassy hills overlooking the Yumeno Fortress. Hidden by eerie darkness, Ushiwakamaru made sure no one exposed themselves to the bright moonlight on the horizon.

"My lord, the Karamete are prepared for your command," Benkei whispered to Ushiwakamaru.

"A surprise rear attack would ensure a quick victory, but the moonlight exposes us. They'll cut us down before we reached the gate." Ushiwakamaru said while squinting. All the men removed their helmets to avoid glare in the clear night.

"Lord Yoritomo will begin his siege at dawn, perhaps we should-," Benkei said before Ushiwakamaru cut him off.

"One can trust in only himself."

"That may be true, my lord, but we still have to clear the plains under clear moonlight and penetrate the front gate. I trust only in the gods," Benkei said.

Suddenly, Thalia ran up to the two men and crouched beside them. "What is happening?"

Ushiwakamaru was startled. "What? Where did you come from? How did you get past my men?"

"This is no place for a girl, Young Sparrow," Benkei said with displeasure.

Thalia smiled and looked at both men. "Fret

not, I can help."

Both men looked at each other and burst into laughter. They shushed each other immediately.

"If I take away the moonlight and the gate, you can win with no harm done to them, correct?" Thalia said while nodding her head gently. She wore an oversized samurai helmet that blocked her vision with each nod.

Ushiwakamaru shrugged. "Yes, but sacrifice is the duty of every samurai."

"Is that so?" Thalia stood and walked slowly towards the castle.

They were a good half-a-mile away, but Ushiwakamaru still worried the Taira would see her. "Get back here!" Ushiwakamaru stood before Benkei shoved him back to the earth.

"You cannot protect her, my lord," Benkei said like a scolding father.

119

Thalia took about fifty paces until she faded away from Ushiwakamaru's and his men vision, swallowed by the darkness. She fell to her knees and dug her fingers into the dirt. Thalia's arms trembled, and sweat began pouring down her face. Black crystal filled her eyeballs as a slight zephyr whirled, though it was not summer. Her arms transformed into tree vines, clutching the earth beneath her. As the sweat dripped to the soil, it created a steam-like gas around her, eventually surrounding her spirit-like form with a heavy fog.

Ushiwakamaru looked in awe as the valley floor began to fill with a dense fog. Even Yumeno Fortress disappeared in its power. Soon, the very unwelcomed moonlight lost its luminosity.

"By the gods," Ushiwakamaru said as he

turned to Benkei. "Prepare the men."

Thalia's arms retracted back to their natural forms, although her eyes remained crystals. She gasped for breath, the air that escaped her when she entered the earth. Covered in the mist of the fog, she shoveled a single hand into the soil, splitting the ground and rumbling the valley. The giant fissure she created split the ground before her until it reached the heavily fortified gate of Yumeno Fortress. In an instant, the giant, wooden gate shattered into a million pieces.

Ushiwakamaru's men streaked past Thalia on horseback with warcries to announce their fierce arrival.

Taira no Kiyomori was a alerted from a deep sleep as two of his most trusted retainers entered his chamber. The Taira commander still donned his evening kimono.

"My lord, we were taken by surprise," a lead retainer shouted. He bowed before Kiyomori as Ushiwakamaru, Benkei, and several of his soldiers stomped into the room. Ushiwakamaru removed the kabuto from his head as the shouts of men battling and fires roaring echoed in the background. Disheveled and soiled, a smile overcame his face. It was his moment to gloat.

"My deepest apologies, my lord," Ushiwakamaru said. "We failed to announce our arrival."

As the fog began to clear, Thalia could see Ushiwakamaru's sigil being raised above the castle walls. As she took a few steps in the castle's direction, a sharp, ghost-like projectile pierced her abdomen, sending the girl to the ground. Thalia screamed from a pain she had never felt before. Regardless of the cloudless night sky, a heavy, muddy rain drenched Thalia.

Ushiwakamaru celebrated with his men in the open courtyard of the castle as Taira men were led away in chains. The rain began to fall heavily, almost flooding the muddy area. Ushiwakamaru stood in silence as he gazed the smoke-filled scene. He wondered if a past battle had ever gone so smooth. Not a single death as a result of his siege. *Was it a coincidence or did Thalia have a hand in this?* Ushiwakamaru was a very spiritual man, but he had never believed in magic, or at least magic for the good of man.

Benkei rode up on his horse and quickly dismounted. "My lord, Lord Yoritomo has taken

Ikuta Castle. We now control Fukuwara!"

Ushiwakamaru nodded and then turned to the main gate, which was shattered into a million pieces, allowing his men to easily take Yumeno Castle. It didn't make sense. *Were the gods that pleased with me?* Suddenly, he realized something or someone was missing. In a panic stare, he said to his loyal retainer and most trusted friend, "Where is Thalia? Bring me my horse!"

Thalia reached as far as she could. Her hand clenched the damp soil as she crawled to safety, where ever that might be. Beyond the pain from the ghostly spear, she felt weak, drained from the use of her inner-energy to create the fog and bring down the wall that could not be brought down. She sobbed as the rain soaked her tunic and her spirit.

"Mother," Thalia called out, hoping Gaia

would come to her rescue. "I am truly the 'lost soul' as you felt. Although I try not to, I have already failed you."

The three wisps floated above Thalia as she struggled to find air in her lungs and strength in her limbs. She tried to lift herself from the ground, but to no avail.

"Foolish girl," the wisps spoke in unison. "You should have known that using the powers bequeathed to you by your mother would open a portal for us."

Thalia spat out crimson blood. Her eyes swelled and her skin began to dry into a thick, leathery husk. "The Spirit of Kalas watches over me," Thalia said in an escaping tone.

All three wisps placed their hands on Thalia, and a surge of ethereal force penetrated Thalia's frame. She screamed from the sharp agony, a cry that could be heard throughout the plains.

"Not on this day, Thalia," the wisps smirked as they flew away.

Gaia was brought to her knees before Gaia. The sky was neither dark or light, but only a gritty color of earth tones and interstellar gases. The line between the surface and the atmosphere disappeared, to which one could not decipher up from down, north from south, reality from dream.

The image of Gaia transformed from Gaia to Nuru, her father she had not seen in so long, at least in human form. The bearded man stood before her with soft eyes, almost resonating sadness with a caring stare. As Nuru started to glow, he soon faded into nothingness. The image of Celio replaced Nuru's. Celio, or at least his form, knelt beside an exhausted Thalia as she began sinking into the damp ground.

"You were created 5,000 years ago. It is the purpose they choose to hide from you," Celio's image said in a monotone voice. "The blolocks are without fear or reason."

Celio then changed into Lady Maiden, Thalia's childhood caregiver for so many centuries. "Only your inner-soul holds the truth, the answer, a gift that Kalas had given to the beasts."

Thalia sunk deeper into the earth.

Lady Maiden became Enlil, the cold uncle Thalia had come to fear. "Alas, your failure is where it will end. Look to yourself for pity. You will not find it anywhere else."

Thalia is nearly smothered by stone and dirt. Only her shoulders and head were above the surface.

Gaia took the place of Enlil. She gave Thalia an empathetic look of despair. "You are no more than what you can endure. It is part of the test."

Thalia was engulfed by the gritty and muddy soil. She took a final breath before surrendering to the elements.

Suffocation. The energy drained from her body. Darkness took over. She could not see, only hear her own muted cries until they disappeared. She calmed herself, breathing when only her lungs allowed. Another limitation of this shell. Thalia's heartbeat slowed. THUMP, THUMP, THUMP...THUMP, THUMP...THUMP. Complete silence until she closed her eyes in the rocky tomb. A single drip of water, repeatedly. Suddenly, she could hear the rivers flowing throughout the world, the wind swirling through mountains, and the growth of flore and fauna.

"I will be what I was meant to be," Thalia
said to herself with determination.

Ushiwakamaru dismounted his horse and
threw his helmet to the ground as soon as he saw
Thalia supine before him. He noticed that she was
pale and not moving. She was like a deflated tree
branch, devoid of any moisture or life.

"You came to me for a reason,"
Ushiwakamaru said as he collapsed to his knees.
"Please do not say goodbye so soon."

Ushiwakamaru began weeping silently
beside Thalia's limp frame. He extended a hand
and gently caressed her normally bronze face. In a
matter of milliseconds, Ushiwakamaru is propelled
several feet into the air, zapped by an energy
source within Thalia. Leaving a trail of smoke and

cinder behind him, Ushiwakamaru landed
unconscious in the bitter field.

12.

Anunnaki Will

Ushiwakamaru opened his eyes slowly to the sounds of swallows chirping in the distance. The sun shined brightly on his pale face. The searing heat was an inviting feeling after such a long sleep. He checked his armor quickly for blood or other markings as he sat up to a smiling Thalia, who was kneeling beside him.

"Thalia, I thought you were-"

"I was no more?" Thalia interrupted. "No, I am very much alive, thanks to you."

Ushiwakamaru noticed she was dressed in a white kimono that almost glistened from the sunlight. A slight zephyr swirled off the ocean to the beach on which Ushiwakamaru found himself. There was a certain peacefulness, beyond the one felt after battle.

"I think... no, I know the gods sent you to me as a sign," Ushiwakamaru said in a begging manner. "You are just a girl, but one day, when you grow older, I want you to be my princess."

Thalia clenched his hand gently and allowed it to ever-so-gently stroke her moist cheek. She smiled and gazed down at the unguarded samurai. "Your mother wants you to know that she misses you very much and watches over her young foal."

A shiver ran through Ushiwakamaru. "I finally now know your purpose, Thalia... to protect me."

"I cannot do for which you will not allow me to do, Ushiwakamaru. Just know, you were never alone."

It is dark and wet. Thalia's ghostly form rose from Ushiwakamaru's unconscious body. It walked to Thalia's lifeless frame, what remained from the wisps attack. Her body and the ghostly figure merged into one. Like the earth that is replenished by liquid mana, Thalia's form began to soften, become more lifelike. She sapped what she needed from the warrior. Thalia turned her head and looked to Ushiwakamaru.

Right on queue, Ushiwakamaru awoke and sat up breathing heavily as the pouring rain washed over his startled face. The heavy sounds of approaching hooves drew his attention. Benkei quickly dismounted as had the seven men behind him.

"My lord! My lord!" Benkei said as he approached Ushiwakamaru. He espied Thalia over his right shoulder. She was slowly lifting herself from the ground, drenched from the rain. Benkei's face was a cocktail of confusion and anger. "My lord, you cannot run off as such! What happened?'

Ushiwakamaru tried to recall the events that had just transpired. He shook his head and stared at Thalia, who was covered in mud.

"My memory escapes me."

The drums echoed throughout the province, and the people danced and cheered. Soldiers armed with wooden swords duelled playfully as they boasted about their triumphs from the battle. Torches glowed and lit up the encampment outside Yumeno Castle. Various foods and drinks found their way to the mouths of those in celebration. The night was young, absent were the thoughts of battles to come. Forgotten were the woes of loss and the fallen.

Celio sat on the floor of the dark chamber deep in the castle. Alone, he stared at the hieroglyphs floating in the air before him. Their glow illuminated the room.

Serenity gave Celio the courage to speak aloud ever so softly. In his native, guttural language, "Eleven-eighty-four, taking place during *Shomu*. More battles to come. Until that day..." Celio paused as his eyes grow bigger. With his hands, Celio manipulated the order of the hieroglyphs. "This story does not end well. Does Thalia know?"

Suddenly, Celio turned to the chamber's entrance. There stood Natto with a tray of bowls for drinking tea. Like a frozen statue, Natto stood there with his mouth agasp. He dropped the tray that came crashing to the floor. They stared frantically into each other's eyes.

"Oops," Celio said nervously.

Thalia and Ushiwakamaru sat across from each other on the tatami mat. Ushiwakamaru lifted a bowl of green tea carefully with two hands and gave it to Thalia. Torches lined the walls, giving the chamber a mystic feel.

"I learned from the master priests at the temple. It is the best green tea in the shogunate. But, I am bias," Ushiwakamaru said followed by a slight smile.

Thalia took the bowl and gave him a nod. She sipped the tea and smiled with satisfaction. "It is very good, Ushi."

Ushiwakamaru took a slow sip from his bowl. "You have to grind the leaves at their earliest stage to capture their true flavor. If you wait too late--"

"He will betray you in the end," Thalia said abruptly.

Ushiwakamaru just stared at her. He dropped his bowl and gritted his teeth. His stern jaw changed into a gentle smile. "I know."

"Ushiwakamaru, you do not truly know who I am or where I come from." Thalia grabbed his hands and held them tightly. "It pains me to not be able to share with you."

Ushiwakamaru chuckled. "He will betray me." Ushiwakamaru pulled his hands away from Thalia. "I know. I know Yoritomo is not to be trusted."

Once again, Thalia held his hands. "Soon, I will have to go. You can come with me."

Ushiwakamaru shook his head. "I cannot.

He is my brother. Don't you understand that, Thalia?"

She did not initially, but soon it came to her. Like Ushiwakamaru, she would never abandon her family, her people. A rush of emotion flooded her chest, bringing tears to her eyes.

"Many times as a boy, I dreamed of joining my brothers in the glory of battle. A day that I never thought would happen is happening now. For the gods, I must embrace this moment," Ushiwakamaru said in a peaceful tone.

"You do not waiver. You are so...pure," Thalia said with a slight smile. She squeezed his hands tightly.

Suddenly, Ushiwakamaru's skin began to transform to a reddish, dull hue. Like ashes from cinder, his flesh began peeling, flames erupting from his pores. Ushiwakamaru closed his eyes as

his slender frame bursted into illustrious flames.
Thalia pulled away. Her hands cupped her mouth
in astonishment.

"Ushiwakamaru!" Thalia said, not knowing
what to do.

Ushiwakamaru opened his eyes and stared
at Thalia with a peaceful glare. Thalia returned his
stare, reaching with a lone hand to offer help,
something. She felt helpless.

"Do not worry, Thalia. This is my destiny,"
Ushiwakamaru said with a smile as the fire grew
even larger. "Do you understand, Thalia?
Thalia?"

"Thalia!" Ushiwakamaru said in a frantic
manner. They still held hands as Thalia awoke
from her daydream or nightmare, depending how
you viewed it. "Are you okay?"

Thalia nodded and gave him a subtle smile

to reassure Ushiwakamaru, not herself. "I am just tired."

Ushiwakamaru stood and bowed to her. "Tomorrow, we leave for Shikoku. The Taira are not finished."

Thalia's gaze continued straight forward. Her eyes looked away from the samurai lord, still mentally searching for the meaning of what she witnessed. That's when the Necklace of Daichi began to glow.

Ushiwakamaru saw the necklace shine but ignored its powerful glare. "I'll see you in the morning." He then left the chamber as air would leave the lungs.

Softly, Thalia said to herself, "Goodbye, Ushi." She stood after a few seconds and made her way out the chamber as well.

It was though Thalia stepped into another dimension. Before her were daylight and a giant waterfall pummeling the rocks below. She felt the warmth of the sun, immediately. The sunlight was almost blinding. Next to the waterfall stood three figures, Celio, Natto and Twilight. As soon as she recognized her cat, she sprinted to them. Twilight leaped into her arms.

"Twilight, where have you been?" Thalia said gleefully. "I missed you."

As though sent through an ethereal plane, "I found a good place to hide." The Abyssinian cat purred while rubbing against Thalia's wet cheek.

Thalia faced Natto. "We are not from this world, my friend. You cannot come with us."

Natto fell to his knees, and his forehead met the ground. "I have nothing left here. My family has left me. I want to go with you."

141

Thalia paused, unsure how to respond. "You will never be able to return."

Natto shook his head vigorously. "I know."

"Then you are a friend," Thalia said with a huge grin. She extended a hand and helped Natto to his feet. "It is time. I have the scroll."

As they walked into the waterfall, Celio and Thalia's wet garments transformed into their native tunics. Thalia held tight to Twilight, letting the waters surround her. Celio followed closely behind.

Just before Natto entered the waterfall, he stopped to espy the scenic planes behind him. With a determined expression, Natto's eyes became mere slits as he transformed into Enlil. "Like I said, I will never leave your side." Then he went.

To be continued...